The Lion Dog
A Sherlock Holmes
Uncovered Tale

Steven Ehrman

ISBN: **1491205091**
ISBN-13: **978-1491205099**

DEDICATION

To my mother who introduced me to the joy of reading
which led to the agony of writing.

CONTENTS

WORKS BY THE SAME AUTHOR

The Sherlock Holmes Uncovered Tales
The Eccentric Painter
The Iron Dog
The Mad Judge
The Spider Web
The Lambs Lane Affair

The Frank Randall Mysteries
The Referral Game
The Visible Suspect

The Zombie Civilization Saga
Zombie Civilization: Genesis
Zombie Civilization: Exodus
Coming Soon:
Zombie Civilization: Numbers

CHAPTER ONE

It was an unnaturally warm spring day of 1889 as I returned to the rooms I shared with my friend Sherlock Holmes at 221B Baker Street. The oppressive atmosphere of heat, combined with Holmes's insistence in playing his own compositions on the violin, had driven me from our humble quarters onto the streets of London. My jaunt had somewhat revived my spirits, and as I ascended the steps of that familiar address, I heard the faint sounds of conversation. As Holmes had been alone at our parting, my curiosity was immediately aroused.

Upon opening the door I was presented with the tableau of two unknown visitors sitting across from Holmes, and apparently in deep conversation that ended abruptly upon my entrance. I felt an acute embarrassment at my interruption.

"My pardon, Holmes," said I. "I see that you have guests. I do not wish to intrude."

"No intrusion at all, doctor, pray be seated," said my friend blandly. "Your return is most fortuitous."

I sat as instructed and studied Holmes's guests. They were a middle-aged man and a somewhat younger woman. The man was of medium height with a ruddy complexion and reddish hair. He was a bit stout, and was dressed in a loud checked jacket. He had an ostentatious pinky ring with a large ruby that he twirled around his finger in an obvious display of affectation.

His companion was an attractive lady with dark hair and fair skin. She was slim of figure and demur in her manner, yet there was fire in her brown eyes. They seemed an odd couple, but they were holding hands in open affection towards one another.

"As I was saying, Watson," continued Holmes. "We have not gotten past introductions and your presence is most welcome. May I present Dr. Watson, my companion and aid in all my cases."

This declaration was met with a look of irritation from the male guest, but I was rewarded with a smile from his female companion.

"Please begin again, Mr. Rutherford," said Holmes.

The ruddy man shifted uncomfortably in his seat and then spoke in a deep baritone with a distinct Australian accent.

"Very well, Mr. Holmes," he began. "I am a plain-spoken man, without university letters, and if you wish this gentleman to be present then that's good enough for me. When I hire a man, I like to give him his head, as it were."

He chuckled slightly at his small joke and his companion patted his hand indulgently.

"But be that as it may, I am Benjamin Rutherford, and this," he said gesturing to the lady, "is my dear wife, Mary." The lady nodded to both Holmes and me. "I find myself in a most difficult spot, Mr. Holmes, and I'm told you're the man capable of helping me."

"You have my full attention," said Holmes.

"Well, it is like this," he began. "I'm a self-made man, you see. I am originally from Australia, as you can probably tell, and I came to London some thirty years ago to make my fortune. I was penniless, yet I had ambition and drive. I found work in the West End as a stagehand. I had no theatrical experience, but I found I had a knack for what people would pay to see. I gradually worked my way up until I found backers to produce my own productions. They were small musical revues at first, but I soon found myself producing several large, and profitable, shows per year."

"My husband has the pulse of the theater patron," said Mrs. Rutherford, in a low voice.

"That's right, gentlemen. I know what the common man wants because I am one. Piccadilly Circus and The Strand theaters aren't filled with the swells, but rather the common folk. I drive my companies hard and keep costs low to make a profit."

"The iron dog," his wife interjected, with a smile.

"What's that?" I asked, somewhat flummoxed.

Rutherford allowed himself a chortle.

"That is a somewhat less than charitable sobriquet, given me by the players in my productions."

"Oh no, Benjamin," protested his wife. "It is one of affection. Why, those actors would not have work were it not for your business acumen."

"Mary is being too kind, gentlemen," said Rutherford. "Why, she herself was a wonderful actress, and imagine her mother was a mere servant. Mary was marvelous in character parts. She was just beginning to get lead roles when she gave that up for marriage."

He seemed almost wistful about her decision. It was not every husband who regrets taking his wife away from her path. My opinion of Benjamin Rutherford was increased by his obvious deep feelings in the matter.

"Mr. Holmes does not want to hear about all that, Benjamin," snapped Mrs. Rutherford. "Please, we came on an unpleasant task, and we should get to it with dispatch lest we lose our nerve."

Rutherford seemed crestfallen at his wife's mild scolding and paused before he continued.

"Quite, quite, my dear. I fear I have gotten astray of my purpose in coming to attend to you, Mr. Holmes. The fact of the matter is that I am being blackmailed, and I want you to put a stop to it."

"Blackmailed, you say?" asked Holmes. "Who precisely is blackmailing you, and what sword do they wield that would cause you to submit?"

Again Rutherford paused and looked to his wife for guidance.

"For goodness sake, Benjamin, we have come this far," said she.

"Right," said he. "In for a penny, in for a pound as they say. The fact is that this woman, Miss Kate Crawley, has certain letters of mine in her possession that she threatens to make public if I do not pay her five hundred pounds."

"Surely such a sum is trivial to you, Mr. Rutherford," said Holmes.

"Why, the sum is not the issue, sir," he cried. "Any payment would be only the beginning. The next demand might be ten times as much or more."

"Agreed," said Holmes. "Although even that might still be worth the cost, depending upon what the letters contain. Pray tell me the details."

"It is just this, Mr. Holmes," Rutherford began. "This Kate Crawley and I were an…well…we were involved while I was still married to my first wife."

"Involved in what manner?" asked Holmes innocently.

"I believe you can infer the manner, sir," said Rutherford in retort. "I concede it was not my finest hour, Holmes. I was a beast. I admit it."

Rutherford buried his face in his hands before regaining control and sitting up straight in his chair.

"Pardon that display, gentlemen, but I am not accustomed to washing my dirty linen in public."

"It is not as scandalous as Benjamin makes it seem," said Mrs. Rutherford. "The first Mrs. Rutherford had been an invalid for many years and was quite insensible to her surroundings. Poor Benjamin simply fell under the spell of a fortune-hunting woman and made a foolish mistake. He broke off the affair when he realized what sort of woman he had become involved with, and his wife mercifully died soon afterwards."

"It was only then that I met Mary," said

Rutherford. "She was a vision and I wanted nothing more than to spend my life with her."

Rutherford's affection for his wife was palpable, but Holmes showed no reaction to his statement of love for his wife other than impatience.

"Of course, of course," said Holmes. "You assume she has kept these letters in her possession to use as a club. It is possible she no longer has the letters and is merely bluffing you with their exposure. Surely it has been many years."

"Would only were that so, Mr. Holmes. Mary, if you please." He motioned to his wife and she produced several letters from her bag. She handed them to her husband, who briefly inspected them, and then he passed them on to Holmes.

Holmes perused the letters in a leisurely manner and then passed them to me. I spied Mrs. Rutherford begin to protest, but she thought better of it and remained silent. I read the letters with a modicum of embarrassment. They were filled with love for "my dearest", and "my angel", and were signed by Rutherford on his personal stationery.

"Why the long delay?" asked Holmes.

"I don't follow your meaning, Mr. Holmes," said Rutherford.

"As you say, this matter had been over for some years, so why has Miss Crawley only now decided to engage in the dicey business of blackmail?"

"Kate has fallen on hard times," said Rutherford.

His wife stirred impatiently at his side and spoke: "Benjamin, it is no use to come to Mr. Holmes and then hold back from him. Please, for both our sakes."

"Of course, you are right, my dear," he agreed. "You see Kate was a fine actress in her day, but as the years passed and her looks faded, she began to find that she was not considered for lead roles any longer. She still thought of herself as an ingénue, but her roles were dwindling down to older character parts. She began drinking heavily. There were several regrettable incidents in which she humiliated herself on stage. Soon the word was spread through the theatrical community, and it is a small one, Mr. Holmes, that she was unreliable, and then even small parts dried up. My understanding is that she leaves her flat now only to obtain drink. Very sad indeed."

"How was the blackmail demand made?" asked Holmes.

"Twice she has accosted me on the street after a show. The first time to make the demand, and the second time to show me that she still had the letters.

9

She said the ones she gave me were only the tip of the iceberg and there's little doubt she has more. What should I do, Mr. Holmes?"

Holmes pulled a pipe from his dressing gown. He tapped it on the table beside him several times and then laid it down.

"My advice to you is to give this matter over to the authorities," said he gravely. "Blackmail is a very messy business indeed, and Scotland Yard is most capable of handling any eventualities that may occur."

"That is quite out of the question," said Rutherford. "I couldn't stand the scandal, Mr. Holmes."

"Mr. Rutherford, as far as I can see, any scandal is one of remote years and surely cannot touch a man of your position today."

"That's just it, Holmes. You see...well, there has been a more recent episode that would likely come to light were this matter to find its way into the papers," explained Rutherford, in a rueful manner. Mrs. Rutherford's cheeks were spotted red with shame and embarrassment. "My wife has forgiven me my errors, but I simply could not put her through a public hearing. Do you see now why we have come to beg your aid?"

I felt a deep warmth for this couple in obvious distress. Rutherford had undoubtedly made mistakes, but he seemed driven to correct them without sullying his wife's reputation. What Holmes felt was unclear, as he displayed no emotion on his countenance. At length he spoke.

"My advice to you remains the same, Mr. Rutherford. I fear I cannot be of aid to you."

"But, Holmes," cried Rutherford. "If it is the matter of your fee, I can pay handsomely, I assure you."

"The fee is not the issue, as my friend, Dr. Watson, could tell you," said he. "I simply do not feel that this matter is one in which I could possibly help, besides the advice of which I have already given you."

Mary Rutherford could no longer restrain herself, and she leaned forward in her seat and spoke, "Don't you see, Mr. Holmes, if you merely spoke to Miss Crawley, and warned her that you were on the case, why, your reputation alone would cause her to rethink her mad enterprise?"

"That may be, madam," returned Holmes. "But my position is unchanged. Good day."

At this Holmes arose in a sign that the interview was at an end. The Rutherfords were not put off that quickly, and argued strenuously with Holmes for some minutes before they finally gave up and exited the room. Holmes settled back into his chair, packed his pipe with his noxious blend of tobacco, and began languidly puffing. I sat and observed my friend for some minutes. It had seemed to me that Holmes was capricious in his denial of aid to the Rutherfords, but I knew my friend well enough to know that he could not be driven from his position. We lapsed into a companionable silence.

CHAPTER TWO

At length Holmes stirred on his couch and addressed me.

"Watson, you have an admirable ability to remain silent, when others would fill the air with their thoughts. It was easily read through your posture during the interview that you believe I should have taken the charge that was offered me. Is that not so?"

"Your affairs are your own, of course, Holmes," I essayed. "But, I admit my heart went out to Mrs. Rutherford and her plight as the faithful wife of a, perhaps undeserving, husband. Would you see her name dragged through the mud?"

"Ah, my friend, as ever you are the champion of the fairer sex. There were some points of interest in the case, but as for the lady, surely she has made her choice and must face the consequences."

"Holmes," I cried. "That is unfair to the lady. Surely it was obvious she is deeply in love with her husband and he her."

"I agree there was a deep love demonstrated here today, yet the entire affair left me uneasy, Watson, and I daresay that perhaps I may reconsider my involvement, after all."

"Why, that is capital, Holmes. A telegram to that effect to the Rutherfords would certainly be a balm for their troubles."

"I did not say I have changed my mind, old friend, merely that I will consider it. Several pipes should be sufficient."

With that Holmes began puffing away and could not be drawn into further conversation. I confined myself to the newspapers, and organized some notes from previous cases with Holmes. There were some fascinating mysteries among them, and the public had been made privy to only a small fraction of them.

The heat intensified through the day as morning turned into afternoon, which gave way to evening. I had fairly drifted off to sleep in my armchair when I was startled by the sound of footsteps on the stairs, and a loud rapping at the door to our rooms.

"Who could that be, Holmes?" asked I.

"A mystery we shall soon solve," said Holmes, as the door was opened and a uniformed sergeant of the police strode into the middle of the room.

"Mr. Sherlock Holmes, I believe," said he, facing my friend.

"I am Sherlock Holmes."

"I have been sent with a message for you, and have been instructed to wait upon your answer, sir," said the sergeant.

With that he thrust a letter into Holmes's hands and stood at attention. Holmes quickly scanned the letter. His eyes were alive with the fire that I knew well.

"What is it, Holmes?" I asked.

"There has been a murder, Watson," said he. "Benjamin Rutherford has been shot and killed in his own study, not an hour ago. Lestrade is on the scene and asks that I attend at once."

I was taken aback. My heart went out to the widow, and I feared her reaction to the tragedy. While I was still in shock, Holmes spoke.

"Tell the good Inspector that Dr. Watson and myself will come at once."

"Yes, sir," said the sergeant. "If you please, we have a hansom waiting for you downstairs."

"Very good, sergeant. We will be down in a moment."

The sergeant neatly saluted and quickly exited the room. His heavy boots thudded on the steps on his way down.

"Am I to go as well, Holmes?" I asked. "It would seem that Lestrade has requested only yourself."

"Watson, I would not dream of entering upon this matter without your aid. Your help may be indispensable. That is, if you are game to come with me."

"I consent, and happily, Holmes. Shall we be off?"

Within minutes we found ourselves in a hansom cab rattling through the streets of London. The Rutherford residence was in a fashionable district close to the West End. Our driver soon pulled to the curb in front of a stolid establishment, and we alighted. The sergeant helped us make our way through a phalanx of police officers into the home. We had no sooner walked through the door, when we were accosted by Inspector Lestrade.

"Mr. Holmes," he cried. "And, of course, Dr. Watson. It is a grisly business, but I am glad to see the both of you."

Lestrade was a dark, terrier-like man. Holmes considered him the best of the Scotland Yard detectives, save perhaps Gregson. I found the man somewhat brusque, although he could be charming at times, but it was true that he admired Holmes's abilities in solving the most obtuse and baffling cases. This had not always been so, but Lestrade had learned through experience not to underestimate Holmes. There was little doubt why we had been called, as the murder suspect had graced our rooms only hours before.

"It is my understanding that Benjamin Rutherford had an interview with you this very day," said Lestrade. "Mrs. Rutherford is upstairs in her bedroom with her doctor, but she has communicated that much."

"It is true," said Holmes. "The Rutherfords offered me a commission this morning, which I did not accept."

"I say, Inspector," said I. "Is the lady's health in danger? Was she assaulted as well?"

"No, doctor. She is merely overcome with the brutality of the crime. It was she who discovered the body, After a short interview, she became overwrought, and her personal physician was sent for. He is with her now, but I expect she will recover after a night's rest."

Lestrade pulled his notebook from his pocket and reviewed it.

"Now, Holmes," he continued. "This commission was, as I understand it, concerned with the attempted blackmail of Rutherford by one Kate Crawley. Is that so?"

"It was, indeed," said he.

"Now surely, Mr. Holmes, you know that that is a matter which should have been brought to the Yard," said Lestrade in a scolding manner. "A bit high handed of you to shield a blackmailer and withhold evidence of a crime from the proper authorities."

I felt my temper rise in defense of my friend. Lestrade's attack on my friend's good name was approaching slander as far as I was concerned, but Holmes seemed blithe in his reply.

"My dear, Inspector," said he. "There was no crime to report, merely the accusation of one and indeed, if it will act as a sop to your sensitivities, I counseled the couple to pursue the matter with the authorities. If they chose not to do so, I can hardly be held at fault."

"Well, I'm certain you followed protocol, as you see it, Mr. Holmes, and I did not mean to suggest otherwise," said Lestrade in a more restrained manner. "It is simply that a murder has occurred within hours of this interview. Can you tell me what transpired at this meeting? The lady could only provide me with a threadbare account owing to her condition."

In his succinct manner, Holmes proceeded to

describe to Lestrade the events of the morning, leaving out nothing that I could discern. The Crawley woman's attempted blackmail of Rutherford with the incriminating letters was included, along with the slightly scandalous matter of Rutherford's infidelity to his current wife. This last item I would have held back as incidental to the case, but Holmes seemed to feel it was important to hold back nothing of note. Lestrade scribbled furiously in his notebook, as Holmes described the meeting, with several grunts of disapproval at the appropriate points.

"Now, Lestrade," said Holmes, as he finished his recitation, "perhaps, you will be good enough to tell the details of the gentleman's death. We have only your note as information so far. Pray give me the facts of the case."

"It would appear fairly straightforward, Holmes," he said. "I have only asked you to appear because of the timing of the murder. The facts are these. At approximately eight this evening Rogers, the butler, admitted a lady to the house. She was described by him as a dark slim woman of middle height. She was veiled, but he noted an Australian accent, and she had a somewhat husky voice. She said her name was Kate Crawley. She asked to see the master. Rogers took her to his master's study, and announced the guest. He retired, and heard nothing else until his mistress began screaming an hour later. She was outside the study and was beside herself, screaming that her husband was dead. She told Rogers that she had thought she had heard a loud noise, possibly the shot, from her bedroom and came down to find her husband stricken. Rogers went into the study and verified that Rutherford was indeed dead, and went into the street to find a constable. One of London's lads was nearby, and he stood guard over the crime scene until I arrived."

"So nothing has been disturbed," said Holmes.

"Only what was necessary to determine that Rutherford was indeed past all hope. A police surgeon examined him earlier, and he was under strict instructions to take care not to disturb the scene. I know your methods, Holmes," said Lestrade. "As I said, this may be a very straightforward matter, but I have learned that when Sherlock Holmes is in the area of a crime, then perhaps all is not as it seems."

As Lestrade finished his speech a man began to descend the stairs. He was a spare, distinguished man carrying a black medical bag. He stopped at the bottom of the stairs to address the Inspector.

"I'll be leaving now, Inspector," he said.

"Very good, doctor," said Lestrade, with gravity. "Allow me to introduce Mr. Sherlock Holmes, and a professional colleague of yours, Dr. Watson. Gentlemen, this is Dr. James Wilson."

The doctor nodded at both of us, and I saw a bit of a flutter in his eyes as the name Sherlock Holmes was announced.

"Mr. Holmes, the detective?" he asked. "I have heard of you, of course, sir. I pray you can bring the perpetrator of this crime to justice."

"Did you know the deceased well, doctor?"

"No, I'm afraid not. I was Mrs. Rutherford's physician. I knew her husband only by reputation. As a denizen of the theater his name was known, if not his face."

"Doctor," said Lestrade. "Will the lady be able to answer any further questions tonight?"

"That will be quite impossible, Inspector," said the doctor, with a weary shake of his head. "I have administered a mild sedative to her, and she is resting now. I will look in on her in the morning. At that time I see no reason why she should not be able to answer your questions. If you gentlemen will excuse me, I will be leaving now. It has been a tiring day for me."

The fatigued doctor excused himself, and Holmes faced Lestrade.

"Inspector, I believe the time has arrived for the inspection of the crime scene. If all has been held as it was, it should be instructive."

"Have you already formed a theory, Holmes?" I asked. His manner was one of tense excitement that I knew well.

"It is dangerous to form an opinion without all the facts, Watson, but there are certain factors that lend themselves to a theory. Time will tell if that theory comes to fruition."

"Well, be that as it may," said Lestrade. "I don't hold myself with fancy theories. Solid detective work and hard toil is good enough for me. Nose to the grindstone if you will, Holmes. This way."

CHAPTER THREE

Lestrade led Holmes and me down a short hallway, and we entered the study of the deceased. The room was very warm. A fire had obviously been lit earlier in the evening and was just dying down. The room was filled with bookshelves lined with tomes and was dominated by a huge mahogany desk. Beside the desk, crumpled on the floor was the dead man.

I immediately recognized the loud checked jacket of Benjamin Rutherford. There was likely not another jacket of that same style in London. Goodness knows, I had never seen one.

The cause of death for the unfortunate gentleman was obvious. There was a bullet wound in the back of his head. It was certainly an entry wound, as it was relatively small. As I walked around the body I was presented with a horribly distorted face. The exit wound had blown out much of Rutherford's forehead and had left the remainder a bloody mess with horribly disfigured features. I had seen many of these types of wounds in Afghanistan, yet I still blanched at the sight of such cruel damage to the human body.

Under the dead man's arm was a sheaf of papers, that appeared to be of the same variety he had shown Holmes and myself that very day. They were undoubtedly the blackmail letters. The hand with the large ruby pinky ring appeared to be clutching reading glasses.

Holmes was examining the body, and I saw that he was paying particular attention to the reading glasses in Rutherford's hand. I followed his interest and saw nothing of note. The glasses were held in a closed fist, and Holmes had produced a magnifying glass from his pocket for a closer inspection. He continued in silence for some time before standing up. He laid his chin upon his chest in deep thought.

"Have you discovered something, Holmes?" asked Lestrade.

"I suppose a large ruby ring of that sort is quite valuable," mused Holmes.

"I see what you are driving at, Mr. Holmes," cried Lestrade. "Perhaps the scene was made to appear to be a crime of blackmail gone wrong when in fact it is a cover for a jewel switch. That ring is certainly worth thousands of pounds. My early information is that it is a trademark of the gentleman."

Ever the man of action, Lestrade eagerly examined the ring. After several minutes he gave a disappointed sigh.

"Nothing there, Holmes," said he. "That ring did not come off tonight. That much is certain. This gentleman was running to stout, and I am confident the ring could not be taken off at all."

I saw at once, Lestrade's point. The ring was encased in flesh on the sides, as rings often are when a man has gained weight whilst continuing to wear it. I could not imagine a criminal managing to pull the ring off of the dead man's finger and replacing it with a fake.

"Nevertheless, Holmes, I will make a note to have the authenticity of the stone checked," averred Lestrade. "Diligence will out, as I've often said."

As much as I admired the methods of Sherlock Holmes, I admit that Lestrade's energy was infectious, and I found myself comparing the two men. Lestrade was the very picture of activity, while Holmes cast a more languid shadow.

"Have you formed an opinion as to how the murder actually took place, Inspector?" asked Holmes. He had strolled over to the dying fire and stood gazing into it.

"Leaving the identity of the killer aside, I believe

the method is easily discernible," said Lestrade, in an officious manner. "The killer gained entrance to the study and, in some manner, induced Rutherford to turn his back to him or her. At that moment the killer shot Rutherford from behind. Probably from a distance of only a few feet."

"Surely not," said Holmes. "Observe the burn marks on the victim's hair. From the scorching, I believe we can deduce that the killer was directly behind Rutherford."

Lestrade and I both leaned down to inspect the body. Holmes was indeed correct; distinct burn marks from the powder were visible.

"Well," said Lestrade, "I will concede that point, but surely it is a minor one. Whether the distance was six feet, ten feet, or point blank, the victim was certainly killed by gunshot."

"A small point, as you say," commented Holmes. "Has the murder weapon been found?"

"It was left beside the body. We were obliged to move it as to determine if it had been recently fired. It is here on the table," said Lestrade.

The Inspector gestured towards a large caliber revolver on a rugged oak table next to a magnificent globe. Holmes picked up the weapon. He sniffed the barrel and felt the weight of the gun and then handed it to me.

"This weapon is familiar to you, I believe," said Holmes.

"Indeed, it is, Holmes," said I, as I examined the piece. "It is an Enfield revolver. This was the standard officer sidearm in Afghanistan. It is an extremely powerful weapon, and is certainly capable of inflicting the massive amount of carnage the victim demonstrates."

"It is a careless killer that leaves the murder weapon at the scene of the crime," said Holmes. "Surely this is a valuable aid in identifying the murderer."

"Not in this case, Holmes," said Lestrade importantly. "The butler identifies it as the belonging to the dead man."

"Indeed; well, that is interesting," said Holmes.

"It makes a certain kind of sense though, Holmes," said Lestrade. "The butler reports that Rutherford kept this gun in his desk, and it was often lying on top of the desk, as his master enjoyed cleaning and oiling it. If that was the case today, then perhaps Rutherford engaged in an argument with someone, the Crawley woman or someone else, and in the heat of the moment, the other person snatches the weapon from his desk and shoots. There is only one round missing. It fits the known facts of the case."

Holmes did not respond, and Lestrade seemed to take Holmes's silence as acquiescence. As I replaced the service revolver on the table, Holmes stirred himself.

"Are you certain that only one round is missing, Lestrade?"

"I am, Holmes. Why do you ask?"

Because right here in the oak paneling, next to the wall there is surely a bullet hole that someone has attempted to cover up."

Holmes drew our attention to a spot on the wall some four feet from the floor. There was indeed a bullet lodged in the wood, and it appeared as if someone had tried to cover it up with a bit of clay. How Holmes had noticed it was quite beyond me.

"Well, I'll make a note of it, Holmes," said Lestrade. "But it does not appear to be a fresh round. I would say it has been there for some time. It's not likely to have anything to do with this crime. Is there anything else you wish?"

"I would like to have a word with the butler now," said Holmes. "If that is convenient to your investigation, Lestrade."

"Of course, Holmes. I know you wish to recover all my ground," said Lestrade, with a good-natured wink.

The butler Rogers was sent for, and he was soon before us. Rogers was a typical English butler. He was slender and of medium height and stood ramrod straight in front of us. He had a taciturn expression on his face, and seemed to mildly disapprove of us being in his master's study.

"Yes, Inspector? May I help you, sir?" said he, cocking his head toward Lestrade. Rogers emphasized the "sir" as if to suggest that a Scotland Yard Inspector was not a proper gentleman.

"This gentleman wishes to ask you some questions. I am instructing you to answer them to your full ability."

"Certainly, sir," he said, and turned to Holmes.

"Now, Rogers, you admitted a woman to this house this evening," stated Holmes, in a low voice.

"I beg your pardon, sir."

Holmes repeated the question in a louder tone of voice.

"That is correct, sir. It was just short of eight o'clock."

"Very good, and had you seen this lady on any previous occasion?" asked Holmes, again in a low tone of voice. Again, the butler asked Holmes to repeat his question and again, Holmes spoke in a loud voice when he repeated it.

"I do not believe the lady was a previous visitor to the house. Of course she was veiled, but I did not recognize the voice and I had not heard that accent before."

"Surely it was the same type of accent your master had."

"I am sorry, sir. I meant that I had never heard a lady's voice with that accent."

"An Australian one, you mean," said Holmes.

"Yes, sir."

"What happened next, Rogers?"

"I announced the lady to the master, and admitted her to the study."

"Did you leave immediately?"

"No, sir. I waited to see if the master had any instructions."

"Did he?"

"No, sir. He dismissed me and I left, closing the door as I went."

"Did your master seem upset by his visitor?"

"Pardon me, sir?"

"Did he seem upset? Surprised? Angry?" demanded Holmes.

"If I may say, the master seemed amused if anything, sir," said Rogers.

"Now I understand there was trouble in the marriage," said Holmes.

"I am sure I would not know, sir," said Rogers stiffly.

"Come now, my good man. This is a murder investigation. I have been told that there was an issue of infidelity in the marriage of your master and mistress."

"I am sure that I could not say, sir," he said. "Will there be anything else?"

"Just a couple more questions. Did you hear anything that could have been the shot that killed Mr. Rutherford?"

"No, sir. You see, I was in the other wing and the study is nearly soundproof. The walls and the doors are quite thick."

"So you heard nothing until Mrs. Rutherford discovered the body?"

"That is correct, sir. The mistress came down from her bedroom, and found the poor master dead. She had nearly fainted by the time I got to her. I found a constable in the street, and attended to her as best I could, until the doctor arrived."

"Was anyone else at home during the tragedy?"

"No, sir. The cook leaves after the evening meal and it is the maid's night off."

"Very good, Rogers," said Holmes. "You may go."

The butler gave a short, stiff bow and left the room.

"Well, his testimony seems quite straightforward, Holmes," said I. "He was obviously lying about Mr. Rutherford's infidelity, but you could hardly expect him to divulge that. Not a butler of the old school such as he."

"That is well observed, Watson," said he. "I did not expect him to confirm it, but his reaction to the question was, as you say, instructive. I am not surprised Rogers did not hear the gunshot," he continued. "Did you notice how hard of hearing the man was?"

"Was that the game you were playing with him, Holmes?" I asked.

"Certainly," said he. "I noticed him cock his head to hear the Inspector. Now the Inspector has a loud voice, and a man with normal hearing should not have had to cock his head to understand him. The fact that he did gave rise to the suspicion that he did not hear well. My small experiment confirmed that."

Whether or not Rogers is hard of hearing is of small import, Holmes," said Lestrade. "The fact is he did not hear it. Why, is surely unimportant."

"As you say," returned Holmes. "I assume you have arrested the Crawley woman."

"We have not as yet," said Lestrade suavely.

"I am surprised by that," said I. "I would have thought that she was the only viable suspect, Inspector."

"We have not ignored that possibility, doctor, but there are facts that have come to my attention that widen the field somewhat," he said. "You have heard of this Iron Dog business, I assume?"

We assented that we had.

"My understanding is that it is not a good-natured nickname, but rather the epithet given to a grasping and ruthless businessman. The early facts suggest that Rutherford has made a myriad of enemies in the past decades. A man such as that might be killed by someone who became aware of this blackmail business, and used it as a cover for a murder to settle an old score."

"Bravo, Lestrade," said Holmes. "That is certainly one possibility."

Holmes seemed surprised at the Inspector's depth of thought in this matter.

"We are not the bumblers you suppose us to be at the Yard, Holmes."

"I think no such thing, Lestrade. I think Scotland Yard is the finest police force in the world. If you have no one with the deduction skills of myself, that does not make the Yard a force of bumblers."

Lestrade thought about that for a moment. He seemed to be unable to discern whether Holmes's statement was a compliment or an insult.

"Well, be that as it may," he continued. "We have Miss Crawley under observation. She can hold while I explore other avenues. If you will excuse me, I intend to interview some of Mr. Rutherford's associates. I doubt many tears are being shed in the West End tonight."

"Good luck, Lestrade," Holmes said.

"I will be in touch, Holmes," said he, and he was off in his normal breakneck manner.

CHAPTER FOUR

We found that the same carriage that had brought us to the Rutherford house was waiting to return us to our lodgings on Baker Street. During our ride, Holmes was deep in thought. I had known my friend long enough to be aware that when he was in that state, that nothing could draw him out. We rode in silence and we presently disembarked at our rooms.

Once inside Holmes curled up in his lounging chair He immediately stuffed his pipe with tobacco he pulled from the toe of a Persian slipper, and began puffing away. Holmes smoked a particularly pungent type of tobacco and the room was soon inundated with it. Although a smoker myself, I walked to the window and threw it open so as to clear the air. The heat of the day was finally dissipating and I settled into my chair. I then opened a book on the naval battles of the War of 1812. The small American navy had, in an unlikely scenario, fought the enormous and proud British navy to a standstill. I was reading an account of one of the most stirring ship-to-ship battles when my eyes grew weary and I laid the book down. My mind had wandered when I heard Holmes speak.

"Regicide is a horrible crime, Watson."

"Indeed, Holmes. It is hard to believe it of Englishmen."

I was shaking my head in sadness when I realized that Holmes had spoken my very thoughts. I looked at my friend and saw the merriment in his eyes.

"Holmes, you villain," I cried. "Did you not promise me after the affair of The Resident Patient that you would refrain from such practical jokes?"

"I apologize, Watson," said he earnestly. "I plead only that the case before us is so stimulating that my skills at detection were bound to find an outlet that was near at hand."

"Well, be that as it may, it is still rather shocking when one finds a voice inside one's own head," said I. "Still I must admit a curiosity at how you managed to pierce my thoughts, and thus intrude upon them. How did you manage it?"

"I was reaching for a fresh bowl for my pipe when I saw you put down your book, deep in thought. I saw, as you set it down, that you were at the pivotal battle between the American frigate USS Constitution and the HMS Guerriere. It was in this battle that the American ship earned her nickname of Old Ironsides. Of course, that nickname is shared by Oliver Cromwell. Your eyes, upon putting down the book, were immediately drawn to the handsome biography of Cromwell by S. R. Gardner that you recently finished. Knowing that Charles I was a personal favorite of yours, I deduced by the sad expression on your face that you were thinking of his foul execution. I then saw you begin to shake your head slowly in disbelief at the actions of our past countrymen. It was then that I commented upon the terrible nature of the crime of regicide. I hope that is clear."

"Outstanding, Holmes," I cried.

"The merest trifle, my dear doctor," said he. "It is a parlour trick, but it is an exercise that keeps the blade of my mind keen."

"Surely the case at hand is exercise enough for your consulting detective skills."

"Yes, the case," said Holmes as if it were a trivial matter. "I have not forgotten the case."

"Have you formed an opinion?" I asked.

Indeed I have, Watson," said he. "But, I require additional information to solve the case."

"Do you intend to interview Kate Crawley, Holmes? It would seem the next step in an orderly investigation."

"Ah, but now you are intruding on my thoughts,

doctor," he said with a laugh. "Miss Crawley is an important cog in this case, and I have not forgotten her. Indeed, I expect that the morning will bring new developments."

What these developments were I could not draw from the taciturn detective and I finally retired to my sleeping chamber, leaving Holmes still on his lounging chair with smoke curled around his head. I fell into a dreamless sleep.

****

I awoke the next morning to bright sunshine streaming through my window. I washed and dressed quickly. My time in the army had accustomed me to a Spartan routine and I was soon ready for my breakfast, which I was certain had already been laid in by the faithful Mrs. Hudson.

I heard the faint sound of voices from the sitting room, which grew into a cacophony when I opened my bedroom door. Advancing into the sitting area, I was surprised to see the room was filled with roughly a dozen street urchins. They were dressed in rags and only their leader was shod. These were the Baker Street Irregulars. They were small group of ragamuffins that Holmes had formed to help facilitate investigations that called for the prying eyes of the London street brigades. In Holmes's opinion, they were worth twice their number in Scotland Yard Inspectors under certain circumstances.

Their leader, a lad named Wiggins whom I recognized from previous cases, stood in front of the line of boys. Wiggins was somewhat older and taller than the rest. He considered himself Holmes's lieutenant, an appellation Holmes encouraged, and he stood at parade line attention in front of my friend.

"Now, Wiggins," said Holmes, as I entered. "The first two charges I have given you are for the entire group. You know the types of establishments to seek out. Do not bother with the expensive ones for either task, but set your men on the seedier ones. You know the type I mean, I am sure."

Right, guv'nor," said Wiggins. "I'll set the boys off proper, I will."

"Good. Now as to the last task, I am entrusting that to you alone, and I want it completed within the hour," said Holmes, and then he turned his attention to the rest of the dirty army. "The regular rates apply, my lads. A shilling a day, per man, with a bonus of a guinea to the lad who completes either task. Success with both tasks would be wonderful, but at least one success is vital. Report to Wiggins, boys, for additional instructions.

Are there any questions?"

"We've got it, we do, sir," said Wiggins, with a wink. "I'll set the lads to the business, and in a day or two it'll be Bob's your uncle."

With that declaration, the small mob streamed from the room. Their footsteps faded upon the stairs and I strolled to the window to see them belch forth from building. With some words from Wiggins that I could not hear, they were soon running down the street and disappeared.

I turned to find Holmes sitting at our table, helping himself to generous portions of the viands of which Mrs. Hudson had provided us. My curiosity at the mission of the Baker Street Irregulars wrestled for some moments with my appetite. In the end my appetite won out. I joined Holmes at the table and ladled a large portion of eggs onto my plate. I followed this with a rasher of bacon, and settled in to break my fast without reserve.

Holmes did not, as a rule, speak of a case when we were dining. Even the informal breakfast table was an oasis from his consulting detective persona. With this in mind, Holmes spoke of a wide variety of topics. I had once made a list of the topics on which he was conversant. It was an eclectic mix of subjects upon which Holmes felt were important to his chosen profession, no matter how tangential the connection was. That morning Holmes spoke on the cross pollination of wild orchids by various insects. It was a fascinating subject to me, and I found that I had quite forgotten about the murder of Benjamin Rutherford, as Holmes held forth on his subject.

"So you see, Watson," said Holmes, as we finished our meal, "though Darwin first made this observation of the benefits of cross pollination, I deem that my research has gone farther still. I believe these studies may dovetail nicely with my beekeeping."

I had often heard Holmes speculate on beekeeping as an avocation during his retirement, but I doubted my old friend's ability to engage in such a dry activity for any measure of time. However, as it was his own future, and not mine, I allowed him to employ his imagination without rebuttal. I did allow myself a small smile as he spoke, which went unnoticed by the great detective as he pontificated. As he drew his lecture to a close, I suddenly remembered the events of the night before and my curiosity of Holmes's conclusions.

"Holmes," said I. "You have been characteristically closed mouthed about the case at hand. Have you nothing to tell me of your thinking?"

"Only that we face a wily killer, Watson. It is possible that the perpetrator of this crime may escape prosecution."

"Surely, not," I cried. "Do you mean to say that you have no leads?"

"Not at all, doctor, but leads and notions have no value in an English court. Even Sherlock Holmes cannot merely accuse. I must have evidence that will bend the minds of twelve stolid Englishmen."

"And do the Irregulars have a task that might inform you of such evidence?"

"That is indeed their charge, Watson. At this very moment my Irregulars are combing the city."

"Then you are certain that they will uncover that which you seek?"

"I am certain of their diligence, but, unfortunately, not of their success. We shall see."

"And you will keep their mission a private matter between you and them?"

"Only for the moment, Watson. Remember, you have seen all that I have seen. It is the evidence of yesterday's events that necessitated the need for the Irregulars."

"You also spoke of an errand especially for Wiggins," I reminded him. "You spoke of confidence that it could be accomplished within the hour."

"Ah, yes," said he. "To Wiggins I gave a special charge. I do not mind telling you, Watson, that it was a personal message to a lady. I asked for an audience, and I expect a reply posthaste."

My thoughts went immediately to Mary Rutherford. I realized Holmes would need to speak with her, but I was shocked at his callousness of demanding a meeting on the morning following her husband's death. Holmes was not reckoned a sentimental man, yet even knowing that, I was of a mind to upbraid him, though I was less than sanguine about the results of such an admonishment. As these thoughts ran through my mind, I heard the bell ring from the downstairs door. The muffled voice of Mrs. Hudson was mingled with another female voice.

"I believe that our guest has arrived, Watson."

CHAPTER FIVE

T he door was flung open, and I saw the figure of Mrs. Hudson.

You have a caller, Mr. Holmes," said she. "And the page is not here at this early hour, as you well know. First your brood of young toughs, and now this?"

"My apologies, Mrs. Hudson," said Holmes. "Necessity is a harsh master. There is murder afoot and time is of the essence."

"A well-spoken gentleman you are, Mr. Holmes," said the landlady, and she stepped to one side so that our caller might enter. "You certainly have honey on your tongue when it suits you."

With that statement Mrs. Hudson left the room, closing the door behind her. To my surprise our visitor was not Mary Rutherford, but rather a woman with whom I was unfamiliar. She had swept into the room with a flourish, but now stood uncertainly before us swaying slightly.

Our visitor was an attractive lady with dark hair

and fair skin. She was slim of figure and had brown eyes and dark hair.

"Please be seated, Miss Crawley," said my friend. "I am Sherlock Holmes, and this is my associate Doctor Watson, who assists me in my investigations."

The lady hesitated, and then sat primly in the chair Holmes had indicated.

"Then you know who I am," said she. "Are you a denizen of the theater?"

"I fear not, dear lady. My friend Watson is a habitué of the West End, but I am not, save for the occasional Wagner opera."

"Then how do you know my name?"

"It requires no great detection skills to surmise that," said he. "You have the carriage and bearing of one trained for the stage, you made a most theatrical entrance just now if I may say so, and of course I sent a message to you within the hour asking for an interview. You have saved me the trip by making the journey yourself, so here we are. My friend and I get few female callers, and seldom one so beautiful."

I was surprised by the last part of Holmes's statement. My friend rarely seemed impressed by female beauty, least of all to comment upon it, but if his aim was flattery it was a success, as Miss Crawley fanned herself and blushed visibly.

"Really, Mr. Holmes," said she with a smile. "I hardly expected such manners from a detective."

"Have you found detectives so distasteful in the past?"

The smile disappeared from her face.

"I have only one detective on which to base my assumptions on the profession as a whole. A horrid little man, who all but accused me of blackmail and murder last evening."

"Ah, so the good Inspector Lestrade made his way to your flat after all," said Holmes.

I smiled at the lady's description of Lestrade. While spoken in a disrespectful manner I nevertheless felt compelled to agree with the substance of her soliloquy. Though thorough, Lestrade's tactics did leave something to be desired in tact.

"Do you then deny, madam, that you were involved in the death of Mr. Benjamin Rutherford last evening?" asked Holmes.

"I do indeed, sir."

"And what of the blackmail attempt?"

The lady appeared flustered and clutched her purse.

"Now, there I am entirely fogged. This Inspector Lestrade said I was attempting to extort money from Ben in exchange for some silly old letters. This is absurd, Mr. Holmes. I am guilty of no such thing, and no lady would ever be involved in anything so seamy."

"But, you do not deny the affair with a man betrothed to another," said Holmes somewhat gently.

"I do not," she said, at length. "Of course, in repose it seems to be a sordid act, but I plead youth and the passion of love. I do not expect others to sympathize."

"I understand the wife was an invalid long past hope," said I. I was rewarded with a wan smile from the lady.

"That is true, doctor. Mrs. Rutherford was a dear person. She was a true patron of the arts; however, she had not recognized a soul in over a year before Ben and I began our affair. He was truly miserable. He loved her, but her essence was gone and the body was a mere vessel of the person that was. He sent me many letters expressing his devotion to me when the affair was only a thought. He finally swept me off my feet, but the guilt was too much for either of us and it lasted only a few weeks. When his wife finally passed, her memory, and our ill deed, kept us apart. When finally he married Mary Dunson, I was happy for both of them."

"You mention the letters," said Holmes. "Do you still possess them?"

"Oh, yes," said she. "The Inspector asked about them last night as well, but with his horrid manner I refused to show them to him."

"But, you still retain them? You are under no obligation to me, my dear, but I counsel you to show them to me. I seek only the truth, and if you are innocent of this foul deed you have nothing to fear from me."

The lady clutched her purse even tighter and appeared to be in a quandary. At length I found her eyes upon me.

"Dr. Watson, you seem a kind and gentle man," said she, in a pleading voice. "Do you advise me to give Mr. Holmes my letters?"

I found myself reddening under her hopeful gaze, as well as the bemused expression on Holmes's face.

"Well...er...well," I stammered. "I have no doubt that you do yourself well by trusting in my companion. You would be in fine hands."

"But, doctor, I understood Mr. Holmes to say

that you were his aid in his investigations, so I would be putting myself in your hands as well. Is that not correct?"

"Of course, my dear," I said, as gallantly as I could.

She studied my words and face, and made a decision.

"It seems as though I must trust someone, and you are both gentlemen, as can be seen by a child. I swear before God that I have killed no one."

The last part of her statement was said with clear conviction, but of course many murderers have made the same statement to Sherlock Holmes only to be ensnared by the brilliance of his detective skills. After pausing for a moment she thrust her hands into her purse and pulled out a sheaf of wrinkled papers. She studied them, her eyes running over the words, and then presented them to Holmes.

Holmes took the letters and studied them carefully. As with the other letters, he employed his magnifying glass for more minute examination. After some minutes he handed the letters to me. They were similar to the letters that Rutherford had shown us. They were written on blank white parchment, and expressed love and devotion to, "My dearest Kate", and to "most lovely Kate".

As I finished my cursory examination of the letters, I returned my attention to Holmes. He was leaning back in his chair with his fingertips from each hand together. Although it appeared that he was nearly dozing, I knew that posture to be indicative of his great intellectual process in motion. The lady and I both waited for Holmes to break the silence.

"You are in a most difficult position, madam," said he. "I expect your arrest at any moment."

"But, Mr. Holmes, I had hoped by sharing all with you that you would be able to shield me from arrest," she cried.

"I had hoped so as well, Miss Crawley, but I fear you have not given me the truth."

The statement was so bald that it took me by surprise. Holmes usually employed the wedge, and not the hammer. I saw that the lady was dumbstruck as well.

"Mr. Holmes, I swear that I did not kill Benjamin Rutherford. That is the truth."

"Had you indeed told me the truth, I may have been able to help you in this moment of need but alas! It is too late now," said he.

"Surely not, Holmes!" I interjected. "Can you not see that this lady is in earnest?"

"I only see what logic and the evidence dictate," said he coldly. "In any case, I hear the well-known footsteps of Inspector Lestrade upon our stairs. The moment for candor is past. Now you are in the hands of Scotland Yard."

As Holmes spoke, I too heard the tread of footsteps approaching our door. In the next moment Inspector Lestrade and two burly sergeants entered the room. Lestrade was the picture of officiousness. He strode quickly by Holmes, and confronted Kate Crawley, as she remained seated.

"Miss Crawley, I have a warrant for your arrest in the blackmail and murder of Benjamin Rutherford," he intoned.

The lady paled visibly, yet remained calm. She stood up and faced the Inspector.

"Do with me as you will, sir, but I say for all to hear that I am guiltless in Benjamin's death."

"That is for English justice to decide, Miss Crawley," said the Inspector. "Any statement you make will be noted. Sergeant, take charge of the prisoner."

The nearest sergeant stepped forward and took Miss Crawley gently by the arm. She maintained a stoic expression and was led from the room with no further words. Lestrade followed her with his eyes and then turned an accusing scowl towards Holmes.

"Why, of all the dwellings in London, did Miss Crawley find her way here?" he asked. "Could it be that you had a message delivered to her, Holmes?"

"If you intend to answer your own questions, Lestrade, then my presence becomes superfluous," said he blandly.

"She has been under observation, and my report is that one of your rapscallions was seen delivering a message that was obviously from you. Do you deny it?"

"I deny nothing, Inspector."

"What was the purpose of this message, Holmes?"

"The purpose was twofold. Firstly, I wished to speak with Miss Crawley and discover her defense against the accusations made against her. She came and she made her defense."

"And what did she say?"

"She denies all. She says she made no extortion attempt and, by extension did not murder Rutherford."

"Of course, she would say that, Holmes," cried Lestrade. "Surely, you are not taken in by a simple denial."

"Perhaps not, but I wished to hear it from the lady's lips."

"You said you had a twofold purpose, Holmes. What was the second?"

"I only wished for my agent Wiggins to observe her rooms and report to me."

"What was his report?"

"He has not reported as of yet. The lady made her way here so quickly she has beaten him to Baker Street, but I believe he is now here."

There was the patter of small footsteps on the stairs, and the diminutive figure of Wiggins burst into the room. The sight of the Inspector brought him up short. He looked a question at Holmes and said nothing.

"I believe that will be all, Lestrade," said Holmes. "I am certain that you have many pressing matters to attend."

Lestrade gave Holmes a grave look.

"So it's to be like that, Holmes?" asked he. "Very well. The Yard needs no help with this crime in any case. Good day, gentlemen."

With those words Lestrade strode from the room.

CHAPTER SIX

"**W**ell, my lad," said Holmes. "I expect that you have a report to make. Out with it, if you will."

The boy shifted uncomfortably on his feet and glanced at me.

"Well, guv'nor, I did just as you said. I handed the lady your note myself."

"Did you observe the room as I instructed?"

"Yes, sir. The sitting room was orderly, it was, sir, and a fire had been lit the night before. It was still warm this morning."

"Very good, Wiggins, now off with you," said Holmes. "I expect you to keep the other lads on the trail, as instructed. Report to me yourself when you have news."

With a tip of his cap Wiggins disappeared from the room, and clattered down the steps. I heard Mrs. Hudson's disapproving voice as he passed her door. Our landlady took a dim view of the Irregulars, as I well knew.

Only her affection for Holmes kept us in home and hearth.

I was thoroughly in the dark. The case against Miss Crawley was strong, yet circumstantial. The only direct testimony against her was the word of a man now dead. Rutherford had vouched no witnesses to the blackmail attempt save himself. His wife was privy only to the letters given as proof that they, and others, existed. Holmes, as was his wont, now lounged back in his chair sending columns of smoke towards the ceiling.

"Do you suppose that Kate Crawley will be convicted in this crime, Holmes?" I asked. "She seemed quite adamant in her defense. I found her story compelling."

"She is certainly a beautiful woman," said Holmes.

"Holmes, I said nothing of beauty," I protested. "It was her testimony on which I was basing my opinion."

"Of course, doctor," said Holmes soothingly. "It was not my intent to suggest otherwise, yet I was struck by her looks."

It was unlike Holmes to essay a comment upon the beauty of a woman. It occurred to me that Holmes was trying to throw me off balance by this unusual comment, so I plowed ahead with my reasoning.

"Could perhaps Lestrade have been right with his theory? Is it possible that a business associate with a grudge took advantage of the situation and murdered Rutherford? It would take fortuitous timing, but it could be done."

My friend stirred himself, emptied his pipe, and replaced it on the table.

"It is a possibility, Watson," said he. "If there is anything to it, I am certain the energetic Lestrade will find evidence of it."

"That seems to me to be the only other possibility, besides Miss Crawley being the culprit."

"On the contrary, Watson. I can imagine fourteen separate theories that fit the facts as we now know them."

"Surely you jest, Holmes," I cried.

"No, my dear doctor. Because the crime appears a certain way, you, and our friend Lestrade, see it only that way. A clever criminal uses such inclinations to advantage."

"I am entirely in the dark, Holmes. You must have observed something that I have not."

"Not at all, doctor. You have seen and heard all that I have. If you do not make use of what you have seen, I am hardly to blame."

This was a typically cryptic comment from Holmes. From our long history together I knew that further questions would not yield further answers. I resolved to keep my own counsel, as well. Holmes had little regard for my own powers of deduction, but I claimed a better understanding of my fellow citizens. It was my hope that the knowledge of humanity would do me in good stead.

The morning papers came and went, and Holmes and I spent the rest of the morning in silent contemplation of the day's news. While Holmes was mainly interested in the agony column and the criminal news of the penny press, I enjoyed perusing the Times in a thorough manner. The pulse of the great city could be felt within the broadsheet pages of the great paper. The news of the day was the usual collection of eclectic events, some sad, some merry, and others simply odd or baffling. A hurricane had ravaged the American coastline, an obscure actor had died of an overdose of sleeping draught, a tragedy at a circus had killed three performers and two spectators, there had been a fire at a Fleet Street publishing house, and an arriving passenger ship from New Zealand had been found to carry smallpox and had been quarantined. These were but a few of the stories that captured my attention.

I attempted to engage Holmes in discussion of

these news events, and was met with a desultory response. As morning waxed into afternoon I found myself feeling quite drowsy, and I slipped into an uneasy sleep. When I awoke I found Holmes scanning the Times and jumping from section to section. At length he arose and began pacing the floor, muttering to himself and smoking furiously. Finally he ceased pacing and seemed to come to a decision.

"I can no longer sit and wait for evidence to come to me, Watson," said he. "There are several avenues of inquiry that I must explore. I may be all day and evening, so do not await supper on my account."

"But, Holmes," I cried. "Can I not accompany you? I am most anxious to find the solution to this foul crime."

"I am sorry, doctor, but it is best that I go alone," said he. Seeing the crestfallen look upon my face he hastened to add, "But, fear not, you do have an important role. While I am gone, Lestrade or Wiggins may return. You are to be my proxy here. If Wiggins returns in my absence, take any message he has precisely. Should the good Inspector make an appearance, use your own wit and judgment to discover what may advance our investigation."

I was indeed disappointed not to be invited to attend with Holmes on his inquiry, but I was gratified to have a function.

"Very well, Holmes. I shall be your eyes and ears here at Baker Street, but can you give some clue as to your thinking?"

Holmes was at the door with his walking stick when he turned towards me with a grim expression on his face.

"The weather is key, Watson. Indeed, had it not been for that I might not have solved the case."

"Then it is solved?" I asked astonished.

"Everything, except for the identity of the murderer."

"Surely, that is not a small item," I cried.

"Indeed not, but I know how the murder was done; now I need to know which of the five people actually committed it."

With that statement, he swept from the room. I was left breathless at his casual announcement that the murder was solved, but the murderer was still unknown. The two statements seemed at odds with one another, but I had learned not to casually dismiss the words of Sherlock Holmes. And what five potential murderers did Holmes have in mind?

I was left to ponder these questions alone for most of the afternoon and into the evening until our page admitted Inspector Lestrade. The Inspector was his normal terrier-like self, but seemed to be a bit agitated.

"And where is Mr. Holmes?" he demanded.

"I have no way of knowing," said I truthfully. "Holmes merely said that he had inquiries to make, and he wished me to remain here in case of visitors."

"Doctor, this is a murder case and I will not play cats-paw for Holmes. I demand you tell me where he has gone."

"Inspector, need I remind you again of the character of Sherlock Holmes? He keeps his own counsel and only shares at the denouement. I have often found it frustrating, but I choose to light a candle rather than curse the darkness."

"Do not quote the Bible to me, doctor."

"It is a Chinese proverb," I said mildly.

"Oh," said Lestrade. "Marvelously clever people, the Chinese. Invented gunpowder, you know."

"I believe so, but that is hardly the point of your visit Inspector."

Lestrade shook his head violently.

"Indeed, it is not. I received a telegram from Holmes informing me that Benjamin Rutherford had a silent partner. It is my understanding that in the theater troubled productions often rely upon an angel, as they say. Holmes identified one, Edward Brown, as the partner. I have just come from questioning him, and he admits the partnership. I had no idea that Rutherford had a partner and Mrs. Rutherford claims no knowledge of one either. How is it that Holmes knows of such matters?"

My mind flew to the Irregulars. Perhaps this was one of the missions Holmes had given them. As I had no direct knowledge, I decided to keep quiet about Holmes's motley army.

"Again, Inspector, I am not privy to the thoughts of Holmes. I swear to you, the name Edward Brown is entirely unknown to me."

Lestrade gazed at me suspiciously, and then his face slowly broadened into a grin.

"Of course, you are right, doctor. I should have known that Holmes would keep you groping in the dark, as well. I admire, I admit, the skill Holmes has shown in solving some very baffling cases, but he has a way of treating the Yard as ribbon clerks."

I did sympathize with Lestrade, and I told him so.

"Is there any message you would like to leave for Holmes?" I asked.

"Just what I have already told you, with one additional fact. Brown has no alibi for the time of the murder. He claims he was strolling through the streets at that hour. It seems to be his custom, and I have no reason to doubt it; but the mere fact that he is an unknown that Holmes is interested in makes me wonder."

I did as well, but I was as fully in the dark about this strange financier as Lestrade. We spoke for some few minutes more, and then the Inspector took his leave and left me to assess this new information. I was certain Holmes already knew everything the Yard did, and that he was simply alerting them to possible suspects. As I was pondering all the permutations of the case, I thought I heard a gentle knock at the door. I had nearly convinced myself that I had imagined it, when it opened and Holmes's lieutenant Wiggins came into the room.

"Doctor, is Mr. Holmes about?" he asked, with less than his usual self-assuredness.

"I am afraid not, Wiggins. He asked me to take any messages for him. You may trust that I will relate any communication to Homes upon his return."

Wiggins shuffled his feet and looked around the room.

"I waited for the constable to leave. Are we alone?"

"We are quite alone, I assure you," said I. I did not bother to correct the lad on Lestrade's rank.

"Mr. Holmes has always said we are to trust you as we would him, so I reckon it's good and proper."

The grimy ragamuffin's tale of Holmes's faith in me warmed my heart, and made me forget the manner in which I had been kept in the dark as to my friend's intentions in the case.

"Speak then, lad."

"Tell Mr. Holmes that we have found one of the men, and he admits the commission. I gave him the note Mr. Holmes had given me and he went pale all over. I got the note back like Mr. Holmes instructed. Here it is."

With a dirty hand, Wiggins thrust the sheet of foolscap at me. The paper was folded twice over so the writing was hidden. I put it in my jacket pocket and returned my attention to the boy.

"Is there anything further, my lad?" I asked.

"Just tell the guv'nor I'll be around tomorrow for Wilson's guinea. He's the one what made the find."

"Very good then, Wiggins. Off you go."

With a smart salute, Wiggins left as silently as the wind across the meadow. I pulled the note from my pocket. I was sorely tempted to open it, but my discretion held me back. Holmes would share it with me when the time was right. I sat it upon the dining table and returned to my chair. I lit a cigarette and watched the smoke curl up towards the ceiling. I soon despaired of Homes returning that night, and I repaired to my bedchamber in preparedness for sleep.

CHAPTER SEVEN

I arose from my sleep at my usual hour and found Holmes at our dining table. He was humming a tune and had begun breakfast without me.

"Join me, Watson," he said. "The day promises much adventure, and we must victual ourselves for the moment."

I needed no encouragement to break my fast. I eagerly assented to Holmes's admonition. Soon I was tucking in a generous portion of the larder provided by our landlady and cook. Holmes avoided all comment on the case, as I expected, and I did not press him upon the point. After a leisurely meal, we made our way to our sitting room. Holmes lit his pipe and I a cigarette. The atmosphere was congenial to conversation.

"Am I to understand, then that the case is at a crucial point?" I asked. "You seem most confident in manner."

"Confident?" Holmes mused. "If so, it is the confidence of the hound who has followed the fox to his den."

"Then the hunt is over?"

"I have several small details yet to arrange, but the trap is set, Watson," said he.

The visit by young Wiggins sprang to my mind.

"Holmes," I cried. "I have a message for you from your Irregulars."

"Ah, yes, doctor. I have already spoken to Wiggins and all is arranged. I tell you, those boys are bloodhounds when a guinea is in the offing."

I was a bit deflated by this statement, as I had hoped to contribute in a material manner to the investigation. Holmes must have seen my expression, for he spoke quickly.

"I do understand, from Mrs. Hudson, that Lestrade was a visitor in my absence. What, pray tell, did the good Inspector want?"

"He has found you were correct as to the partnership between Rutherford and this Edward Brown. He seemed quite put out that you had discovered this without his aid. Quite put out indeed, Holmes."

"Lestrade never learns that many people become quite closed mouthed with the police, and most especially theater people. I learned more lounging in the stalls, and backstage, in a day than the Yard could

73

possibly discover in a month."

"I take it you made these inquiries incognito."

"You would be correct in that assumption, doctor. I posed alternately as an agent and as an out-of-work stagehand. Once I was established as of the guild, tongues loosened and information ran as does water."

"What is the agenda for the day, Holmes?" I asked.

"I have several telegrams out that I expect answer to, and from them we can accordingly set our plans. I believe all will be done with by the end of this day."

"So soon, Holmes?" I cried. "You are a magician."

"Nothing of the sort, doctor, I merely follow the facts where they lead me, and do not attempt to twist the facts to fit any particular theory. This case has taken several unexpected courses, but all is now in order."

"From whom are you now awaiting responses?"

"There are several parties, but the first one, I believe, has chosen to answer in person. I perceive that is the step of Lestrade."

No sooner had these words escaped the mouth

of Holmes, than Lestrade was admitted by our page. He looked to be in a surly mood, and curtly nodded to each of us.

"Holmes, what is the meaning of this?" he asked, shaking a telegram in his hands. "Do you seriously ask me to bring a prisoner from gaol to a meeting at the scene of the very crime of which she stands accused? My word, Holmes, I am blessed if I haven't given you your head before, but this is the absolute limit."

"It is merely a request, Lestrade," said Holmes soothingly. "Should you choose to deny it, you would certainly be within your rights, but I believe it is in your self-interest to grant me this request. Mrs. Rutherford had already consented to host the doctor and myself."

"Does she know that the Crawley woman will be there?" asked Lestrade suspiciously.

"I do not believe that it came up," said Holmes blandly.

"I can believe that, Holmes."

"It may be somewhat of a surprise, but once it is presented as a *fait accompli* I am certain she will acquiesce."

Lestrade was silent for a moment as he considered Holmes's words. It was indeed an audacious request by my old friend, but Lestrade was well aware of the tremendous abilities of Holmes. The pull between caution and curiosity was played out on the Inspector's countenance.

"Very well, Holmes," he said finally. "I shall do as you say and I, and the prisoner, will be there at the appointed hour."

"Splendid," said Holmes. "I promise that you will not regret it, Lestrade."

"As you say, Holmes. Well, I'm off. Remain seated, doctor, I can find my own way out."

With those words the Inspector left, and Holmes reached for his violin.

"So I am to attend this meeting as well, Holmes," said I, as he drew his bow across the strings.

"Of course, doctor. Where would Johnson be without Boswell? You shall most certainly attend. In fact, your presence will be quite necessary."

"Will all five of your suspects be there?" I asked.

"Only four, doctor. One of the five is dead."

"What?" I gasped. "Do you mean to say that you suspect Rutherford in his own death?"

Instead of answering, Holmes began playing his violin. A strange melody emanated from his instrument that was both soothing and alternately jarring. Noting his inattention to all but his composition, I abandoned further inquiries and determined to wait until the evening hours during which the meeting was to occur.

****

Several more telegrams arrived for Holmes during the day, but he would not be drawn out further. The telegrams seemed to elevate his mood, so I took it that his program was intact. Towards eight o'clock we engaged a hansom, and began our short journey to the Rutherford residence.

The night was growing foggy as we descended our cab. The tendrils of the grey mist covered the Rutherford home. Though not quite a genuine London pea souper, it was very thick and the home only came fully into view as we approached it. I felt a chill in spite of the warm weather. Holmes rang the bell and I heard measured steps approaching. At length the door was opened, and the visage of Rogers, the butler, appeared.

"I believe we are expected, my man," said Holmes.

"Yes, sir," he intoned. "The mistress is indeed expecting you, sirs. Please follow me."

Rogers led the way in his stately, ramrod-stiff manner, and we followed. To my surprise, Rogers led us into the study. The room was empty, but I could still see the form of Benjamin Rutherford lying cruelly murdered in my mind. I sat on a chair near a window, and Holmes began pacing. Our host was nowhere to be seen as of yet. Holmes was near the desk, when he came to attention gazing over my shoulder.

"Watson," he cried. "Is there a figure staring in from outside?"

I leapt up, and flew to the window. I fumbled with the latch, and finally managed to open it. I threw the window outward and peered into the foggy darkness. I could see and hear nothing of note. I soon found Holmes at my shoulder.

"If there was someone, Holmes, I fear we have missed them," said I.

"Perhaps it is unimportant at any rate, doctor," he said evenly. "I believe our host is approaching."

Within moments Mrs. Rutherford made her appearance. She carried herself in a dignified manner. I bowed to the lady. Holmes greeted her as well, with a curt nod, and she sat primly at her deceased husband's desk.

"Mr. Holmes, I hope you can explain this

somewhat surprising request," said she. "This house is still in mourning."

"I do regret, madam, the intrusion, but I assure you that it is of the highest urgency."

"Very well, Mr. Holmes. Please proceed."

"Unfortunately our numbers are not complete, but I hear the bell so perhaps that is the remainder of our party."

Mary Rutherford's face evinced some surprise at the announcement of more guests, but she remained stoic and waited. Presently, Inspector Lestrade was ushered into the study. He was accompanied by two police sergeants, Kate Crawley, and a tall-distinguished man with whom I was unacquainted. Holmes had a quiet word with Rogers, and the butler remained by the door with a puzzled expression.

"What is that woman doing here?" cried Mary Rutherford.

"She is here at my urging, and with the permission of the Yard. Our other visitor is your deceased husband's silent partner, Edward Brown."

The tall man gave a small nod, and took a seat on the couch. Kate Crawley sat on the same couch, somewhat apart from him, and folded her hands on her lap. Lestrade remained standing.

"I have heard some talk of this man being poor Benjamin's partner, but I know nothing of it," said Mrs. Rutherford.

"I am certain his relationship with your husband was unknown to you, but his *bona fides* can be easily proven," said Holmes. "Is that not true, Mr. Brown?"

The tall man shifted uncomfortably, but looked directly at Holmes and Mary Rutherford in turn.

"That is true, Mr. Holmes. Ben Rutherford and I have been equal partners for some years now. I have the right to buy out his half at a nominal cost in the event of his death, as he had the right in the event of mine." He looked steadily at the dismayed face of Mary Rutherford. "But I would not dream of impoverishing a widow in such a mean way, no matter the contract. We will agree on a fair price."

Mary Rutherford had seemed stunned at the first part of Brown's statement, but she brightened as he finished.

"This is all too much for me," she said, fanning herself. "I do not know quite what to say."

"The monetary matters can be easily cleared up, but there is still the murder to consider," said Holmes.

"But surely, Mr. Holmes, the killer of my husband sits on that sofa," cried Mary Rutherford.

"Perhaps," said Holmes.

"I did not kill Ben,' said Kate Crawley quietly.

"This is your show, Holmes," said Lestrade. "Please make your point. I have taken more than a small chance bringing the prisoner here."

"Very well," said Holmes. "As the murderer is in the room, we can proceed."

CHAPTER EIGHT

A ripple of excitement ran through the room.

Mary Rutherford was fanning herself furiously. Kate Crawley had a worried expression. Only Edward Brown maintained a serene air. Even Rogers lost a bit of his stoic facade. A frown crossed Lestrade's face, but he restrained himself from interfering.

"From the beginning, this entire crime had a theatrical atmosphere," began Holmes. "This is perhaps not surprising since so many of the players are from the theater. Benjamin Rutherford was a producer of plays; his wife, Mary Rutherford, was a former actress, as I learned at our first meeting; Kate Crawley is an actress; and even Mr. Edward Brown is a player from behind the curtains. There is another player who has trod the boards, but we will come back to that person.

"When the Rutherfords visited me on Baker Street, they ostensibly came seeking my help, but they also told an interesting story that myself, and my good friend Dr. Watson, could bear witness to. That was that they were under assault by a former paramour of

Benjamin Rutherford. A lady who threatened to expose Rutherford as an adulterer, unless paid handsomely. I do not believe it is breaking any confidences to say that Miss Kate Crawley was named as the blackmailer."

"We know all this, Holmes," said Lestrade restlessly, as he sat down.

"Indeed, sir. This has been common knowledge. By heavens, I see no reason to rehash the whole matter in front of the grieving widow," said Brown.

"If you will indulge me further, I believe I can make your expense of time well worth your troubles," said Holmes. "Now, Watson and I had the couple under close observation during this interview, and that very same day we received notice from the Inspector that Benjamin Rutherford lay dead in his study. In this very study."

Holmes halted and studied the faces of the men and women gathered. I did as well, but could see nothing of note, save a bit of hope in Kate Crawley's face. Holmes continued.

"There were several items of note in the room. First was the wound. It was a shot in the back of the head. Powder burns demonstrated that it was a point-blank shot fired from a gun the deceased was known to keep in his desk, and even on top of the desk. How do you reconstruct the crime, Lestrade?"

"Why, it is simple, Holmes. The killer, either Miss Crawley or someone else, persuaded Rutherford to turn his back to them and then snatched the gun from the desk and shot him."

"Precisely," said Holmes. "Now, Inspector, is it your experience that men turn their backs on blackmailers, or any enemy, with a gun in full view?"

"Why, no, Holmes. By heavens, they do not!" he cried.

"That was merely the first item of note. The next oddity concerns the weather."

"I beg your pardon, Holmes. Did you say the weather was odd?" asked Lestrade. "It was unbearably hot. Surely, that is not unusual for summer."

"It is not, but building a fire during a heat wave is." said Holmes placidly. "There had been a fire lit in this room, but to what purpose? The existence of the fire was another clue something was amiss at the scene. I now draw your attention to the body. What was the identity of the dead man? Watson, I ask you."

Holmes startled me with a direct question and I hesitated in answer.

"Why, surely it was Benjamin Rutherford," said I. "Who else?"

"Who else, indeed," said Holmes, "But the face was horribly disfigured, so by what means did you identify him?"

"Why, Holmes, we had seen the gentleman only hours before the crime. There cannot be two checked jackets like his in the city, and he wore a very distinctive ruby ring," said I.

"Holmes, what is this rubbish?" cried Lestrade. "Do you seriously mean to suggest that the body was of some other person? Mrs. Rutherford, was the man killed in this study your husband?"

"It was, Inspector," she said calmly.

"And you, Rogers. You knew the man for many years. Is there any doubt in your mind that the dead man was your master, Benjamin Rutherford?"

"None at all, sir," said the taciturn butler. "It was the master. I could not possibly be mistaken."

"Well, there you have it, Holmes," said Lestrade, with some venom. "I believe we have taken up enough of these good people's time."

With that, Lestrade made as if to rise, but a gesture from Holmes halted him. Despite his doubts, the power of Sherlock Holmes's manner overawed him momentarily. Holmes took advantage of the juncture and continued.

"My dear Inspector, I did not mean that the dead man was not Rutherford. I meant only that most any man of a similar body type might appear to be Benjamin Rutherford to someone who had never met him. Watson, cast your mind back to our meeting with the Rutherfords."

I did as requested, and closed my eyes in attention to the task.

"Did Mr. Rutherford have any nervous tic, or affectation?"

I pictured the bluff man in his loud checked jacket sitting next to his demur wife. What was it that he had done? And then it came to me in a flash.

"Why, of course, Holmes. I see what you are driving at. Rutherford continually spun his ring around his finger. He likely was unaware he was even doing it. Many of us have such habits. What of it?"

"I examined the hand of the dead man closely, and even drew attention to it," said Holmes. "Lestrade, you saw the finger the ring was on."

"I did, Mr. Holmes," said Lestrade. "The ring was embedded on the finger, such as when a man wears a ring and gains weight over the years."

"Could that ring have been spun around the finger as Watson described?"

Lestrade shook his head reluctantly, and I saw in my memory the finger clearly. I was shocked at the implication, and once again found myself admiring Holmes's power of observation.

"It could not have been," said Lestrade slowly. "Are you saying what I think you are saying, Holmes?"

"I am indeed, Inspector. The man presented to Watson and myself as Benjamin Rutherford was in fact an imposter."

All eyes turned to Mary Rutherford, but she maintained a regal bearing and said nothing.

"Holmes, how long have you known this?" asked Lestrade.

"I suspected something was amiss at that first meeting. The erstwhile Rutherford made some curious comments. He very sadly described his wife's exit from the stage, and specifically said she left 'for marriage'. He did not say to marry him, just for marriage. He also mentioned that she was a former actress herself, and that she came from the servant class. Mrs. Rutherford rebuked him strongly for this aside, as these were matters she did not wish brought to the forefront. However, as I was unfamiliar with either party, I put these down as mere curiosities. It was only when murder was committed that they loomed larger in my mind."

"Mrs. Rutherford, how do you answer these charges?" growled Lestrade.

The lady sat primly behind the desk, and smoothed her dress. At length she looked up, and spoke.

"I have heard no charges, Inspector," said she.

"But what answer do you have for this business with the ring?"

"Mr. Holmes and his friend are mistaken," she said, in a collected voice. "I remember no such affectation with poor Ben's ring."

Lestrade seemed to be put somewhat off his stride by the lady's placid demeanor. A short chuckle from Holmes startled everyone. He gained control of his mirth quickly.

"Madam, you are truly a joy to joust with, but there is more."

Holmes walked to the window, and opened it.

"I have invited another guest," said he. "I believe that is his knock at the door. Rogers, please remain. Lestrade, could send one of the sergeants to admit our new guest?"

With a nod from Lestrade, a tall police sergeant exited the room. He soon returned with a young lad and a wizened old man dressed in a faded coat and battered hat. The young boy was none other than Wiggins.

"He's here just as you wished, guv'nor," said Wiggins, with a large grin, and a side look at the Inspector.

"Very good, Wiggins," said Holmes. "You may leave."

In a trice Wiggins was gone, and the elderly man stood awkwardly by himself, kneading his hat in his hands.

"What is your name and profession, my good man?" asked Holmes.

"I'm Parson," said the man, with a nod at the group. "I have a small jewelry repair shop. It has been mine since my father passed on over thirty years ago."

"Quite right," said Holmes. He turned his attention back to the rest of the gathered folk. "Now, if the Rutherford whom Watson and I met was an imposter, he had to be equipped with the accoutrements that would identify him as Benjamin Rutherford. Accordingly I sent my agents out to scour the less-reputable tailor and jewelry shops in order to find who might have manufactured the checked jacket and a reasonable replica of the Rutherford ruby ring. The tailor could not be discovered, but Parson here was." Holmes turned back to the elflike jeweler. "Now, Parson, did you make an imitation ruby ring recently?"

"I did, sir."

"Who commissioned it?"

"A lady did, sir."

"Is the lady in question in the room?"

"Indeed, she is, sir. That is her, and no mistake."

Parson pointed a bony finger at Mary Rutherford. The lady remained remarkably composed, and said nothing.

"Are you certain?" demanded Lestrade.

The old man trembled under Lestrade's gaze, but he shook his head yes violently.

"It was her, sir. It is not often I receive a lady in my humble shop. I'll swear to it."

"Very well," said Lestrade. "Sergeant, hold this man outside. We will need to take a statement from him."

Parson, with a cringing bow, left the room with the police officer.

"Well, madam?" said Holmes to Mrs. Rutherford. "What say you?"

"That man is mistaken also, Mr. Holmes," she said. "He is a mere tradesman, after all. Surely his word means nothing against mine."

"Well, we shall see," said Holmes. "At any rate, I believe we have established that a charade was played for my benefit. I, Sherlock Homes, could testify that Benjamin Rutherford was being blackmailed. His death afterwards would surely be connected to that blackmail attempt, but was it?"

"What do you mean, Holmes?" I asked bewildered. "Do you mean Kate Crawley left the man alive, and some other wrongdoer killed Rutherford hoping to throw suspicion on her?"

Holmes paced across the room for some minutes before answering. Lestrade seemed about to speak on several occasions, but mastered himself and waited for Holmes to resume. Finally, the detective halted and spoke.

"There were several suspects I considered," he said. "The first was the person who impersonated Rutherford, but I struck him from the list. The second was Kate Crawley, but I quickly was satisfied that she was not the killer. The third was the business partner of Benjamin Rutherford, Edward Brown."

"Now, really," interrupted Brown. "This is slanderous, sir."

"Compose yourself, Mr. Brown," said Holmes. "You were eliminated just as Miss Crawley was, and by the same testimony of the same person. That person was the fourth suspect."

"What person, Holmes?" I asked excitedly.

"Rogers, the butler."

"Rogers? What could be his motive, Holmes?" asked Lestrade.

"You forget the conversation I had with the impersonator. He mentioned that Mary Rutherford was from the servant class. I thought it possible that Rogers and Mrs. Rutherford might have a long and hidden association. Perhaps even a family relationship."

"I swear it is not true, Mr. Holmes," said Rogers, losing his composure. "I had never met the mistress before Mr. Rutherford brought her into this house."

"I know that now, Rogers. I have had your antecedents thoroughly examined. I am satisfied that there was no previous relationship. In fact, it was your statement to me that made the solution to the case possible."

"What did Rogers say that had any bearing on

the identity of the murderer?" I asked. I racked my brain trying to think of something from his statement that had important evidence, but could not.

"Tell us, Holmes," said Lestrade. "I must admit that I noticed nothing of import in Rogers's statement. As I recall it was quite straightforward. He let in a veiled woman with an Australian accent, and admitted her to his master's den. There does not seem to be much to divine from that. He never declared he could identify Miss Crawley, if that's what you are driving at."

"No, not any of that, Inspector. Recall I asked Rogers what his master's attitude had been when he admitted the woman. I asked if Rutherford had seemed upset, or surprised, or angry. He replied that Rutherford seemed amused. That was the key."

"Holmes, I am still at sea," said I. "What did Rutherford's attitude tell you?'

"It told me that Rutherford saw through the disguise that his butler did not. He recognized his wife, despite the accent and the veil. He smiled and sent Rogers away, because what was there to fear from his loving spouse? It is my speculation that she had made a wager with her husband that she could fool Rogers with a disguise. Remember, the false Rutherford told us she was very good in character parts, and character roles often involve an accent. At any rate, once inside I am certain she removed the veil and in some way maneuvered her husband into turning his back to her, and then fired the deadly round. She was counting on Rogers's deafness. With the thick walls, she was reasonably sure he would not hear. I believe she had a trial run in which she fired a round into the oak paneling. That was the round we discovered, Lestrade. If Rogers had heard, and come running the day she ran her test, she could always say the gun had discharged accidentally. We can assume the test was successful because she went ahead with her very audacious plan."

"What of the fire, Holmes? You said it was important," I reminded him.

"Ah, the fire. I believe that Mrs. Rutherford came that night wearing another dress under the outward dress. That dress and the veil must disappear. After all, the police would likely search the house. So as soon as the murder was done, she built a fire and threw the dress and veil in. I looked at the dying fire and attempted to discern remnants of the material, but they had been entirely consumed."

"So there never was a blackmail attempt, Holmes?" I asked.

"No, Watson. Miss Crawley showed us her letters, and they were markedly different. They used her real name, instead of diminutive pet names, such as on the other notes, and they were not written on Rutherford's letterhead. As Rutherford was engaging in behavior he hoped to keep secret, he would hardly use his own stationery. No, the extortion attempt was a fabrication employed by Mrs. Rutherford and her accomplice. Is all this correct so far, Mrs. Rutherford?"

Mary Rutherford had a look that conveyed both scorn and amusement.

"It is a very pretty tale, Mr. Holmes, but I still maintain that I know nothing of the fiction you have created," she said with confidence. "I believe that you and the doctor are mistaken about my husband's ring, and as for that jeweler," she wrinkled her nose in disgust, "I doubt anyone will believe his word over mine."

If the words were intended to deflate Holmes, they did not have the desired result. He merely shook his head sadly.

"Madam, I admire your fortitude, but the game is up," said he. Holmes thrust his hands in his pockets and turned to me. "Watson, do you recall attempting to interest me in various news events from the Times recently?"

"Of course, Holmes," said I. "There was a hurricane in America and a smallpox outbreak on a ship. I am sorry, I do not recollect the others."

"Thankfully, I have a somewhat better recall of our conversation. The one item that struck me was the tragic death of an English actor from an overdose of sleeping draught. As it happened, he was found dead the evening of the Rutherford murder. When he did not make an appearance at the theater, his company went to his rooms and found him dead. His name was Peter Fennell."

"But, surely, Holmes, that was before the murder," said Lestrade. "What does that tragedy have to do with this case?"

"I believe I can tell you that, Inspector," said Holmes. From his inside pocket my friend pulled out what appeared to be a playbill of some sort. "This is the program of the play that Peter Fennell was a member of. His picture appears on the back. Watson, would you look at this picture, and tell me if you have seen this gentleman before."

I took the program from Holmes's outstretched hand. Turning it over to the picture of Fennell, I saw at once what Holmes meant.

"Why, it is the man who was presented to us as Benjamin Rutherford," I cried. "The duplicate as well as the original died the same night."

"And by the same hand, doctor," said Holmes. "Mary Rutherford needed a confederate to pull off this scheme, but she meant to share her spoils with no one. After they had played their scene at Baker Street, they retired to his rooms. I suspect they shared a celebratory glass of wine, which Mrs. Rutherford dosed with sleeping draught. By the time she murdered her husband, Peter Fennell was already dead. Fennell was an old associate of Mrs. Rutherford, and no doubt she used her considerable charms in order to entice him into this plot. He paid with his life for his weakness. Madam, do you have any reply now? The case is complete and I believe that Inspector Lestrade will have some additional questions for you at the Yard."

"That's right, Mrs. Rutherford," said Lestrade, as he rose from his seat. He was the embodiment of officiousness. "You will most certainly have to accompany me."

Mary Rutherford was crying softly by this point. She was leaning over the desk sobbing. As she collected herself she sat up, and in the same motion opened the top drawer to the desk. In a flash, a large revolver was in her hands, pointing at Holmes.

"I knew we should not have chosen you, but Peter insisted," she hissed. "That folly is now in the past, but I have another act yet before this curtain closes. If you gentlemen will excuse me, I will make my exit."

The room was frozen. I glanced at Lestrade, and

he was in a state of shock. I feared for the life of Holmes, as the glint of hatred toward him was palpable from the woman. Holmes alone did not seem nonplussed by the drawn weapon.

"The third act is finished, Mrs. Rutherford," he said, as he walked slowly towards her. "The gun will be of no avail to you, and you will leave this room only to be arrested."

"Stay where you are," she snarled. "I will shoot if I must."

Holmes continued walking slowly towards her. He was only a single pace away from her as I tensed to leap to his aid. At that very moment the lady pulled the trigger on the service revolver. There was a loud click as the hammer came down, but there was no explosion. I felt my heart nearly stop, but Holmes merely smiled. Mary Rutherford had a look of disbelief on her face. She pulled the trigger twice more in quick succession. She went limp, and sank back into her chair. The gun clattered to the floor, and Holmes bent to retrieve it. I went quickly to his side.

"My word, Holmes, that was nervy of you," said I. "What if the gun had been loaded?"

"But it was loaded when we arrived, doctor. I am sure that Mrs. Rutherford made certain of that. She is too clever a criminal to leave a weapon she may need unloaded. However, I suspected it and unloaded the gun myself after we arrived."

Holmes pulled a handful of cartridges from his pocket. I recognized the .476 rounds at once.

"But, how, Holmes?" I asked. "I was with you the entire time. How did you manage to unload the weapon?"

"Do you recall the figure I saw at the window, doctor? I fear I must tell you that was a ruse in order that I might unload the revolver without your knowledge. I am sorry, my old friend, but I desired to play a lone hand."

"I am capable of keeping a secret, Holmes. Dash it all, but you are close at times. In the future you might give me the benefit of the doubt."

"I will certainly keep that in mind, doctor," said Holmes, with a twinkle. "Believe me, Watson, without your stalwart support I do not know what I would do."

"Well, be that as it may, I do congratulate you, Holmes. This was a splendid demonstration of your skills."

"Please, doctor, my modesty," said he, in a thoroughly unconvincing manner. "Now I believe that Lestrade has a duty to perform."

We stepped aside as Lestrade took the arm of a now truly weeping Mary Rutherford. After a quick word with Holmes, he exited, taking with him Kate Crawley. He explained she was to be released naturally, but that it was necessary for her to return with him. Holmes and I said our goodbyes all around, and returned to our humble lodgings for the night.

CHAPTER NINE

The morning broke on a cooler day than we had had in several weeks. I welcomed the respite, and sat down to breakfast. Holmes was unpredictable in the morning. Some days he was a quite early riser, and on others he would miss the morning meal altogether. On this day he joined me soon after I had begun, and we passed a pleasant meal with pleasing conversation. The end of a case sometimes left Holmes at sixes and sevens. His agile mind required activity, and I worried when leisure hours were spread before him. However, despite my fears, the ending of the case had left him in high spirits. We were relaxing over coffee and cigarettes when our page announced we had guests.

"Whom do you suppose is calling, Holmes?" I asked.

"It is undoubtedly Lestrade and the charming Miss Crawley," said Holmes. "I requested they attend to us this morning. I wish to know the state of Mary Rutherford, and also to see how Miss Crawley has weathered this storm."

It pained me that I had quite forgotten the trial that Kate Crawley had been through, and I was delighted when I saw the bright expression on her face as she and Lestrade entered. Holmes and I seated our guests and saw to their needs. Miss Crawley accepted a biscuit, and Lestrade happily took possession of a fine cigar, a box of which Holmes had earned from Sir Henry Farnsworth as a gift for clearing up a small matter. As our guests reclined in the comfort of our sitting room, I found myself very much drawn to Kate Crawley. In spite of her ordeal she seemed more beautiful and composed than when she had first appeared before us. It occurred to me that her stay in gaol had robbed her of the ability to obtain strong drink, and her constitution was recovering as a result. Regardless of the cause, she was a handsome woman.

"Well, Lestrade, how is Mrs. Rutherford finding her new rooms?" asked Holmes. "I hope the change was not too deleterious to her tastes."

"Don't worry about that one, Holmes," chuckled Lestrade. "She is a tigress, ready to blow out her own brains or those of anyone else. I believe that she is quite mad."

"Madness, Lestrade?" I asked. "Do you mean she may be found not responsible for her actions?"

"Not at all, doctor. I merely mean that she is

determined to take down all around her if she must go down. She has cast a wide net. She claims that Rogers did it so that he would inherit, but that is outrageous. Rutherford's will explicitly names several secondary beneficiaries. All of them are relations in Australia. Rogers couldn't possibly hope to inherit. She says Miss Crawley here was the actual blackmailer, despite her having the original letters in her possession. She has also thrown Edward Brown's name into the mix, making a bizarre set of accusations of fiduciary malfeasance, despite his being the silent partner. They are mere ravings. She is guilty by her own words. She is now simply attempting to muddy the water. As a woman she may escape the hangman's noose, but she will certainly face prison walls until her death."

The final words of Lestrade were harsh, but I could not help, but to find myself in sympathy with them. Holmes continued to smoke, and Kate Crawley was nibbling on her biscuit with seemingly little appetite.

"Holmes," continued Lestrade. "I find myself in your debt in this matter. I was outfoxed by the Rutherford woman and I am man enough to admit I was on entirely the wrong trail. You prevented a miscarriage of justice."

"I did little," said Holmes, with a wave of his hand. "Remember, Lestrade, I had the advantage of meeting the false Benjamin Rutherford. As I said last night there were signs of duplicity at the time, but since no crime had occurred I did not pursue my instincts. Had you been here, you may have had the same inklings."

Lestrade smiled at the compliment from Holmes. I myself doubted Holmes's theory. I could not see the stolid Scotland Yard Inspector divining the murder plot by the subtle clues Holmes had noticed, but if the great man was willing to apply a salve to Lestrade's wounded ego, it was his to do.

"Why, that is a capital thing to say, Holmes," beamed the Inspector. "I must say however, that there does not seem to be great deal of sadness at Rutherford's passing among the people I interviewed in this investigation. From stagehands to stockbrokers, I received a portrait of a terribly hard businessman who was loved by few. Not that he deserved to die, of course, but there you have it."

"What of the players in the productions that Rutherford was backing?" I asked. "Are they to be thrown to the streets?"

"No, doctor," said the Inspector. "Mr. Edward Brown has stepped into Rutherford's shoes. He tells me that he had been a silent partner too long and he now wishes to step to the fore. He has even offered Miss Crawley here a part in a new musical that is currently being put together. It sounds quite the saucy role, eh,

Miss Crawley?"

The woman blushed under the Inspector's words.

"It is true that Mr. Brown has been most kind. It seems he remembers me from before my...well, troubles began. I will make good on this opportunity. It seems heaven-sent, gentlemen. I feel I have all of you to thank for this, and especially you, Mr. Holmes. Without you I would be languishing in a prison cell this very moment. How can I thank you?"

Homes smiled at the lady, but returned no words. I saw that Lestrade was beginning to stir, and I sensed that he wished to be on his way. As if reading my thoughts, Lestrade arose.

"Holmes, I must be off. The duty of an Inspector for the Yard allows no laxity. Miss Crawley, by all rights you deserve a conveyance home, as it was Scotland Yard which took you from it. May I see you there myself?"

Lestrade bowed with more grace and good manners than I gave him credit for. The lady gave every sign of accepting his offer, when Holmes intervened.

"Lestrade, if I may presume. I wish to speak to Miss Crawley. I assure you that I will see that she makes it safely back to her flat, if she will consent to stay for a bit further."

"Why, of course, Mr. Holmes," she said. "I am in your debt, after all."

The Inspector left, and the three of us resumed our seats. Holmes fixed his gaze upon Miss Crawley and did not speak for some moments.

"Now, my dear, I suppose you know why I wanted to speak with you privately," he said blandly.

"Why, no, Mr. Holmes. I am quite at sea. Is there some way I can be of aid to you?"

"No, but I can be of aid to you. I ask you to consider the escape from justice that you have had. I hope this close call will compel you to make a better choice for your future. Should I hear otherwise, I may be obliged to acquaint the good Inspector with what you and I both know."

I could not for the life of me divine Holmes's meaning, but the expression on Kate Crawley's face gave evidence of an untold truth.

"How did you know?" she asked in a whisper. "I swear it is all like a nightmare now. How I could ever have thought to blackmail Ben I do not know."

"You mean Miss Crawley actually was blackmailing Rutherford?" I asked. "But, Holmes, you proved that it was all Mary Rutherford's doing."

"I proved nothing of the sort, doctor. It was, of course Mary Rutherford's idea to commit murder, but the fuse was lit by the opportunity she saw when Miss Crawley began her extortion attempt. I believe she wanted Rutherford himself to meet with me. That would have done away with the dangerous fiction of disguising Peter Fennell, but Rutherford did not see Miss Crawley as a genuine menace. He knew that she may threaten when she was in her cups, but that she was not the type of person to follow through on her threats."

"But, Holmes, what of the letters Miss Crawley gave you? You noted immediately the use of her name and the lack of Rutherford's stationery."

"It was clever ruse from a desperate woman, Watson. When the Inspector alerted her to the trouble she was in, she created a new set of letters. She burned the old letters. I asked Wiggins to check for evidence of a fire and he found it when he delivered my note. Again, we have a fire in the middle of a heat wave, Watson. She made certain the new letters were different from the ones she had given Rutherford. It made no sense that he was reluctant to use his stationary because of possible scandal. They were signed with his name. It was a forgery by Miss Crawley, but it put to the lie the notion he was afraid they would fall into the wrong hands. Additionally, the letters appeared to be wrinkled with age, but, Watson, is that how women retain old love letters? Do they allow them to become wrinkled? Of course not. If they are kept at all, they are pressed in a book. These letters were brand-new and then wrinkled by Miss Crawley to simulate age. Is that not all correct, madam?

"It is, Mr. Holmes," she said in a clear voice. "What will you have me do?"

"Make a clean break with your recent past. Do not allow your judgment to be colored by drink. Melancholy is a dangerous state to be in, and it is exacerbated by strong spirits. Take the lifeline that has been thrown to you, and resume your career. The lady who protested her innocence in this room deserves to trod the boards. That is where your acting talent should have free rein. You shall never have another chance to redeem yourself as you have had this day."

The lady hesitated not a moment. She stood up and faced Holmes.

"You shall never have cause to regret this, Mr. Holmes."

"Very well," said Holmes. "May the doctor , and I, accompany you home. I did promise Lestrade I would see to it."

"No thank you," said she. "I wish to walk in the sun. Good day to you, gentlemen. Please be my guests when the new show opens."

With that she made a stately exit. Holmes and I found ourselves alone. My head was still spinning, but Holmes simply reached for his Persian slipper and removed some of his finest shag from the toe. He lit his pipe in some contentment.

"Do you disapprove of my actions here, Watson? You are most quiet."

"I heartily approve, Holmes. I am merely agog at this final turn. This is the final turn, isn't it?" I asked, with some suspicion.

"The hunt is over, my old friend. I think we have earned at least one day's rest from our toils."

"Agreed, but, Holmes, why did you allow Miss Crawley to escape justice?"

"The answer is twofold. Firstly, I judge her character to be a good one. She had a moral lapse, but I do not believe that she could have followed through to an actual crime. Apparently Rutherford felt the same. Secondly, I judge the character of Benjamin Rutherford in a much harsher light. Lestrade reported that Rutherford's death brought little mourning, and that was my finding as well. In my tramp through the theater district, I found much rejoicing at his death. One woman threw her life away in the destruction of the man, but I saw no reason to throw away the life of another. Miss Crawley will always remember this, and that will keep her on the path of right."

We lapsed into silence after that. Holmes persisted in his pipe, and I reviewed the case in my mind. Something was gnawing at me. It suddenly struck me what it was.

"Holmes," I said, in a voice dripping with satisfaction. "Although you did manage to solve the case, it occurs to me that even though you suspected something was amiss with the Rutherfords when they visited, you were still fooled. You accepted the ersatz Benjamin Rutherford as the real person. That is actually most extraordinary."

"You forget, Watson, that I had never met Benjamin Rutherford. Anyone reasonably close to his physical type would appear to be Rutherford. Anything else troubling you, doctor?"

"But, Holmes, what of the accent? Benjamin Rutherford was born and raised in Australia. The actor Peter Fennel was an Englishman. I must admit I am shocked that he was able to fool Sherlock Holmes with an affected accent."

I had played my final trump card, and I was certain that, for once, I had bested Holmes. It was with a smug satisfaction that I leaned back in my chair to observe his reply. It was not long in coming.

"The answer to that is quite simple, Watson. I have learned that although Peter Fennel was born in England, he spent two years in Australia, from age four to six. These are the formative language years in regard to accents. I have written a slight monograph on the subject. That fact, doubtless, explains his mastery of the Australian accent."

"That is a flimsy thread for an argument, Holmes," said I, with no little sarcasm.

"Ah, but the most magnificent tapestry began as a humble thread," said my friend blithely. "Now I believe the muse is upon me. Would you please hand me my violin, Watson?"

The End

Special Note

If you've read and enjoyed The Sherlock Holmes Uncovered Tales please add a review at the site on which you purchased it. Reviews help sales, of course, but they also provide a guide for those attempting to find books they might enjoy. A review from a reader, rather than the author or publisher, is often more reassuring to the potential reader because it comes from an unbiased source.

Thank you,

Steven Ehrman